Jade the Gem Dragon

Melody Lockhart

This edition published in 2021 by Arcturus Publishing Limited
26/27 Bickels Yard, 151–153 Bermondsey Street,
London SE1 3HA

Author: Melody Lockhart
Illustrator: Morgan Huff
Editors: Annabel Savery, Joe Harris and Donna Gregory
Designers: Jeni Child and Rosie Bellwood

CH007646NT
Supplier 10, Date 0121, Print run 10893

Printed in the UK

MIX
Paper from
responsible sources
FSC   FSC® C018072
www.fsc.org

Contents

Chapter 1
A New Arrival

"There's no such thing as a pair of shoes with two left feet. Give it here!"

"It's not a left foot! It's just upside down! And you've got *my* sock! And stop pushing!"

Kat watched her younger brothers as they started wrestling each other again. They bumped into the coat stand in the hallway, which fell over with a loud crash. The cats bolted upstairs, and the baby started crying.

"Jordan! Jayden! For the last time!" shouted their mother from the kitchen.

Kat was sitting on the bottom step in the hallway. No one even noticed she was there!

Kat's home had never been calm, but recently things had gone up a gear—from busy, to frantic. Chaotic, even.

Ever since baby Brianna had arrived, her six-year-old twin brothers had been out of control. Any energy that her mother had left after dealing with Brianna was soaked up by them. Dad had been working night shifts at the hospital, and when he got home, all he seemed to do was play with the baby.

It seemed like nobody had any time for Kat. Which was why she had made it through to 2pm on a Saturday without a single person speaking to her.

Her mother came through into the hallway, rocking back and forth as she cradled the new baby. She looked tired.

"How have you still not got your coats on, boys?" she said. Kat had been ready to go for the last ten minutes. "At this rate, the market will be closed by the time we get there!"

Kat took a deep breath. "Mama," she said, "is it okay if I head over to Rosie's instead?"

As if on cue, Brianna's screaming got even louder. Her mother answered without looking up, "Sure, hon. Have fun."

By the time Kat reached Rosie's house, Willow Cottage, she felt very glum indeed. Rosie was her best friend in the world—and on seeing Kat's face, Rosie put her hand on her shoulder. "What's up?" she asked gently.

"My home is like a zoo," said Kat, "and I'm not just talking about the animals." Kat's family did have a lot of pets. With two cats, four hamsters, an iguana, six chickens, and three kids, there was barely room for a baby!

Rosie nodded. "It'll get better—I promise."

"Yeah," said Kat with a forced smile. "I hope so. Anyway, shall we go to the vets?"

"Hello, Kat!" Rosie's mother came out of the front door. "I'm going to the library, Rosie. What are you two up to today? Wait, let me guess—going to Starfall Forest again!"

"Yes!" smiled Rosie, "to see the magical vets who take care of sick unicorns and dragons!"

Rosie's mother chuckled. "Just be back for dinner," she said, strolling down the path.

Kat smiled. "She doesn't believe you then?"

"No," said Rosie. "But she thinks I have a great imagination!"

The two girls walked around the side of the house, through the overgrown yard behind it, and into the forest.

As they got deeper into the woods, a dozen fluffy creatures with bear-like faces floated up from the bushes, carried aloft on tiny wings. "Flutterpuffs!" cried Rosie. They bobbed up and down around the girls, making excited squeaks and whistles. A coral-pink creature got tangled in Kat's dark, curly hair.

Kat couldn't help but laugh as she untangled it. The animals always made her feel better. The girls walked on, soon coming across the path to the vets' surgery.

"You know," said Rosie, "every time my Dad comes into the forest, he suddenly remembers something he's forgotten to do, and dashes back to the house."

"Calico Comfrey's special enchantment," said Kat, "to keep adults away."

Calico Comfrey was a wizard. A hundred years ago, he had made the forest a safe haven for magical creatures, and built a surgery to take care of them. "Yes," said Rosie. "It's funny though—Dad keeps on coming back."

"Do you think maybe he remembers playing here as a kid?" said Kat.

The girls reached a huge oak tree. Kat pressed a lump on the trunk, and with a creak, the bark split and parted like curtains—revealing a door-like opening.

As they stepped inside and began to descend the spiral staircase, the girls were greeted by a bellowing noise. They exchanged a puzzled look. At the bottom of the steps were several doors. Kat pushed one open.

"Just in time, my dearies!" cried a friendly voice. "Quick, I need help to get this flappopotamus' tooth out!"

The voice belonged to Doctor Hart, who was the vet in charge of Calico Comfrey's. She was also Calico's granddaughter.

As Kat and Rosie entered the room, they found Doctor Hart with her head right inside a large animal's mouth. The creature, which looked like a hippo with tiny wings, let out another great bellow.

"Stop it," said Doctor Hart, firmly, from inside its mouth. "All that grumbling won't help one bit."

Then she straightened up and turned to the girls. "I was in the Mazewood all morning gathering herbs, and I got totally lost. Fortunately, a friendly forest creature— a collywobble—led me back. But in the time that I was gone, all my tools vanished!"

As she spoke, a tiny animal peeked out from behind a cupboard in the corner of

the room. It looked a little like a purple hedgehog with tiny, curly horns. Doctor Hart's eyes narrowed. "Ah-ha!" she cried. "I should have known. Girls, this is a hodgepodge. He will have taken my tools to his nest."

The hodgepodge pattered over to Kat, sniffed her, then began to shimmy up her leg with its sticky little feet. "Hodgepodges love magical things," said Doctor Hart. "He'll be after the crystalzoometer in your pocket."

"Do you want this?" asked Kat, taking out the zoometer—a magical device given to her by the vets. The zoometer pointed toward magical animals in the same way that a magnet points to north. The hodgepodge nodded so hard its horns wobbled.

"Well, I'm afraid I can't let you have it, but if you show me where your nest is, I'll give you something even better." She patted the other pocket. "I'll give you what's in *here*."

The hodgepodge gazed hard at her, tilting its head to one side as if in deep thought. Finally, it gave a little nod and ran toward the door, beckoning Kat to follow. "Come on!" Kat called to Doctor Hart and Rosie.

The creature led them out into the forest, and to the trunk of a tall beech tree. It jumped up and down, pointing at the branches and chattering excitedly. Up in the tree, crawling busily through the branches, were more hodgepodges, as well as what looked like some messy bird nests.

"Well done!" exclaimed Doctor Hart. "Lots of things go missing from the surgery, but we can't usually find the hodgepodges' nests because they move them to different spots every day. Hodgepodges can dig and climb, so we don't even know whether to start looking underground or in the treetops!"

From somewhere below ground they heard a deep grumbling noise. "That's the flappopotamus calling out in pain!" cried Doctor Hart. "Her tooth hurts, poor thing!"

"I'll be quick!" said Kat, taking a deep breath before climbing into the tree, her knee bumping on the rough bark. In her pockets were some coins, a pocket mirror, and a few chocolates in shiny wrappers. Her plan was to try to trade them for Doctor Hart's tools.

"Be careful, Kat!" called Rosie and Doctor Hart from below. The hodgepodge led Kat past lots of other nests, right to the top of the tree. Then it sat down proudly in front of a large nest. It held its hands open wide to show off its handiwork.

"I'm impressed, little guy," said Kat. "Show me what you've taken from the surgery and we'll do a trade."

The hodgepodge thought for a moment, then dived into its nest. Kat edged closer, catching sight of a wobbly pile of bracelets, rings, keys, picture frames, headphones, and sports trophies. Kat spotted a silver spoon that looked suspiciously like one she had used at Rosie's house.

The hodgepodge rummaged among its treasures, then jumped up happily. It was holding a pair of dentist's forceps!

"The tools are all here!" shouted Kat. "As well as lots of things that don't look magical at all."

"I shouldn't presume, dearie," called Doctor Hart. "The most ordinary-looking things can have a little magic in them!"

"Here we go then, Mister Hodgepodge—pass me everything you took today and I'll give you all of these."

Kat emptied her pockets and held out her items to the creature. The hodgepodge snuffled forward, opened the mirror, and stared into it. It began pulling funny faces. Then, the hodgepodge threw the coins into

its nest and unwrapped a chocolate. As it tasted the treat, delight spread across its face.

Kat called down to Rosie and Doctor Hart: "I think I might have found something that hodgepodges like even more than magical treasure!"

Then the hodgepodge slowly, and very reluctantly, picked up Doctor Hart's forceps and passed them to Kat.

"Please may I have that spoon as well?" Kat asked. The hodgepodge looked fondly at the spoon for a second, then handed it over.

"Thank you!" she smiled, placing both items in her coat pocket. Then she carefully climbed down the tree, branch by branch.

"Amazing!" said Doctor Hart as Kat reached the ground.

Rosie laughed: "That's my dad's cereal spoon—he's been looking everywhere for it!"

"Let's get back," said Doctor Hart, "and sort out the poor flappopotamus!"

They raced back to the surgery, where they found the flappopotamus lying on its side, groaning. Doctor Hart rolled up her sleeves, then gently pulled open the creature's huge mouth. Kat and Rosie watched in amazement as the vet leaned right inside, reaching toward the rotten tooth with her forceps.

"That's going to smart," said Rosie.

"Oh, not at all!" said Doctor Hart. "These are my magical *feel-no-pain* forceps."

Just then, the creature let out a deafening, hot, and smelly burp. "Poor Doctor Hart!" giggled Rosie. The doctor's head was still deep in the creature's mouth. The girls held their noses but leaned in to watch—after all, they were trainee vets now, and they wanted to learn how to take care of the animals.

After a few twists and a couple of hard tugs, the large molar came loose.

"There we go!" cried Doctor Hart. She was breathing heavily from the effort. "It's out!"

She rinsed the tooth, then showed Rosie and Kat. The flappopotamus sat up, and the tiny wings on its back began to beat rapidly back and forth. Kat and Rosie gasped as it rose unsteadily into the air and did a sort of clumsy dance. It was definitely feeling better!

"Right then, my dearies," said Doctor Hart. "I'd better get packing. I'm off to Gnome Town to check on the newborn grufflegoats."

"Oh no—not more babies!" whispered Kat to Rosie, wrinkling her nose. She thought of noisy baby Brianna at home.

"What are grufflegoats?" asked Rosie.

"They're cheeky little creatures with the most wonderful wool," said Doctor Hart. "The wool changes shade depending on a grufflegoat's mood, which helps the gnomes

take care of them. The gnomes knit it into sweaters, to keep them warm in the mines."

"The sweaters must get pretty sooty down in the mines," said Rosie.

"Oh no, they don't mine coal," said Doctor Hart. "They mine mystical crystals."

"Mystical crysticals!" said Kat, making Rosie burst out laughing.

"The crysticals—the crystals, I mean—can do all kinds of useful things. We use them to power magical machines like your zoometer ... and our ambulance."

"The magic carpet!" the girls chorused.

Rosie gave Kat a nudge and a smile. "A new adventure!" said Rosie. "That's what you need to take your mind off things. It's just what the doctor ordered."

"The doctor?" said Kat. "I think you mean the magical vet!"

Chapter 2
A Case of Dragon Flu

"*C*an we come with you?" asked Kat.

Doctor Hart smiled kindly. "Why yes, of course you can."

Kat and Rosie followed her through the twisting passages of the veterinary surgery and up a long, winding staircase. At the top, they found a room where dozens of pipes belched rainbow smoke and bubbles.

In the middle of the room floated a woven carpet. A young woman with round glasses was fiddling with the little engine attached to one end of it.

"Hello, Doctor Clarice!" chorused the girls.

"Hello, sweethearts," said Doctor Clarice. As well as being one of the surgery's vets, Clarice was very good at fixing machines. "That's the squeaky valve fixed. The carpet should run smoothly now—until its crystal power runs out, that is."

The carpet rippled as Doctor Hart, Kat, and Rosie stepped onto it. Clarice pulled a lever on the engine, and the carpet jumped forward with a pop, rushing toward a closed door. At the last possible moment, the door burst open, and they found themselves hurtling through the open air.

The carpet raced over Starfall Forest, leaving a trail of rainbow bubbles behind it. The girls watched the treetops rushing by, looking like scribbles from a green crayon.

They soared over the Mazewood, where the trees moved around whenever you weren't looking straight at them. Earlier in the summer, Rosie and Kat had met a unicorn there. They had named her Oona.

As they passed over a river, Rosie tapped Kat's shoulder and pointed. Kat's jaw dropped. They were looking at a waterfall—except that the water was flowing the wrong way.

"A waterclimb!" she exclaimed.

"We're nearly there now," said Doctor Hart. "Next stop: Gnome Town."

That's when Kat saw the purple smoke. It was billowing up from a group of trees just on the other side of the river.

"Well now," said Doctor Hart, redirecting the magic carpet toward the sparkling smoke, "I think we might make a detour before we visit our friends the gnomes. Is that okay, girls?"

"Of course—but what is it?" asked Rosie.

"That's dragon's breath," said Doctor Hart. A dragon definitely shouldn't be in this part of the forest at this time of day. Why has it left its cave?"

As they got closer to the smoke, Doctor
Hart explained that dragons had lived in
the caves at Cottontop Mountains for as
long as anyone could remember. "It's their
home," she said. "It really is a terrible sign
for one to leave. My grandfather would be
beside himself."

Doctor Hart lowered the magic carpet
to the forest floor. "The best way to approach
a dragon is to pretend it is a cat ... let it
come to you."

Doctor Hart led Rosie and Kat toward
the source of the smoke, and soon a beautiful,
green-scaled dragon came into view. It was
curled up tightly with its eyes half-closed.

When the dragon saw Doctor Hart, Kat,
and Rosie, it lifted its head slightly, let out
a huff of thick, violet smoke, then rolled
over onto its back.

"That's a good sign!" said Doctor Hart. "We can go closer!"

They walked over slowly, not wanting to startle the creature. Doctor Hart led the way. The vet knelt down at the dragon's head and began tickling under its chin. The dragon stretched out its body, wriggled its legs, and made a happy-sounding sigh.

"Kat, Rosie ... " said Doctor Hart, "slowly kneel down and stroke the dragon's belly."

As soon as they touched the dragon's scales, it began to purr. The girls smiled at each other.

"It really is just like a cat!" said Kat.

Suddenly, the creature gave a tremendous sneeze. The girls jumped back as flames shot out of its nose. Doctor Hart looked alarmed.

"Dragons should never sneeze! She must have dragon flu," gasped Doctor Hart.

"Dragons get flu?" asked Rosie.

"Rarely—but yes. And it can be pretty serious, especially for the younger ones. Unfortunately, I can't treat it here."

Kat looked at Rosie, her eyes wide with worry. "We should take her straight back to the surgery," said Kat, "and come back to Gnome Town some other time."

"Good thinking!" said Doctor Hart, as she scurried off to fetch the carpet. When she returned, Kat and Rosie worked together to lift the sick dragon onto it. Then Doctor Hart started the carpet up again, making it rise into the air, gently this time.

On the way back to the surgery, the engine began to make a worrying gurgling noise.

"Ah," said Doctor Hart. "That can't be good. I think the crystal fuel must be running out."

The carpet lurched and spluttered the rest of the way. It eventually landed in the vets' garage with a heavy thud.

"Oh my goodness!" said Doctor Clarice. She was standing in the doorway, stroking some flutterpuffs. "Is the carpet okay?"

"Worry about that later," said Doctor Hart. "First things first—this dragon needs our help. I think she has the flu."

Doctor Clarice looked shocked. "Quick—let's get her inside." They all worked together to get the dragon indoors, supporting her as she took wobbly steps. When they finally got her into Doctor Clarice's lab, the little dragon collapsed from the effort.

Doctor Hart built a large fire to keep the dragon warm, while Doctor Clarice carried out an examination. "Runny nose, check. Weakness, check. Fever, check."

The dragon sneezed sharply, singeing the bottom of Doctor Hart's coat. Then it began to shiver.

"This is certainly dragon flu. Lots of fluids for the poor thing," said Doctor Hart, taking off her slightly burned coat. "We'll need to stay nearby to make sure she doesn't get worse."

"Worse?" said Rosie. "What could happen?"

"In the worst cases of dragon flu," continued Doctor Hart, "dragons can lose their ability to fly."

"Oh that's terrible!" gasped Kat.

"Don't worry," said Doctor Hart, kindly. "We'll take care of her. But now it's time for you girls to get home—it's been a long day."

Rosie and Kat looked at their watches and realized it truly was time to head home.

"Oh yes, we need to hurry back," said Rosie. She gave the sleeping dragon a gentle pat. "But before we go, she needs a name, doesn't she?"

"Yes," said Kat, thinking for a moment. "I know," she said, "let's call her Jade—like the green gem. Because of her green scales."

Everyone agreed this was a perfect name. Kat and Rosie said goodbye and wound their way home through the trees.

As they entered Rosie's garden, a striped, rabbit-like creature hopped toward them. "A honeybunny!" said Kat. She knelt down to stroke its soft fur, thinking of poor Jade.

"What a day!" said Rosie.

"I know!" said Kat, just as a happy thought popped into her head. "But it's not over yet. Dad and I are going to see the new *Ultra Girl* movie tonight. Everyone's been so busy recently, but he promised he'd make the time. I can almost smell the popcorn!"

Kat jogged the rest of the way home. As she opened the front door, she prepared herself for the chaos of the crying baby and scrapping twins, but surprisingly, the house was quiet. She walked down the hall, calling "Hello!" but there was no answer until she reached the family room.

"Shhhh, Kat!" whispered her dad. He was sitting on the sofa with baby Brianna.

He looked very tired. "I've finally got the baby to sleep, and your mother is napping upstairs. The boys are playing video games. Can you make sure all the animals have been fed?"

Kat felt a prod of doubt. "But we are still going to see the movie, aren't we?" she asked, dreading the answer.

"I'm sorry, no. Not tonight. I need to do some work later—and I really need Brianna to sleep until then, so your mother can rest."

"But you promised!" Kat yelled angrily. "Why do you never play with *me* anymore? I wish I didn't *have* a baby sister!" As soon as the horrible words were out of her mouth, Kat realized there was no taking them back.

She ran to her bedroom and buried herself under her bedcovers. Hot tears rolled down her cheeks. She heard a loud wailing from downstairs. She'd woken baby Brianna.

Chapter 3
Crystal Crisis

The next morning, Jordan and Jayden flicked cereal at each other over the breakfast table, but at least baby Brianna wasn't crying. She sat in her bouncy chair while their mother fixed breakfast. Kat's unkind words from last night buzzed around inside her head. She reached out a finger to touch Brianna's arm. Quick as a flash, the baby grabbed her big sister's finger in her tiny fist.

Brianna gave Kat a beautiful, gummy smile. Kat couldn't help but grin back.

Rosie popped her head round the open back door. "Coming, Kat?" she said.

Kat didn't need to be asked twice. The girls walked quickly through the forest, keen to see how Jade the dragon was doing. They passed the place where the flutterpuffs gathered, reached the tree where the vets worked, and knocked on the part of the bark that let them into the the vets' surgery.

As they stepped through the entrance, they bumped into a little gnome coming the other way. Doctor Morel was another magical vet who worked at the surgery.

"Oh my spoons and jars," he cried grumpily, adjusting the mushrooms that grew from his hat. "You girls really should watch where you're going!"

"Sorry, Doctor Morel," they chorused as they rushed to Doctor Clarice's lab.

Jade the dragon was sleeping in the corner of the lab, snoring noisily. When Kat and Rosie entered the room, the little dragon opened one eye and huffed contentedly.

Doctor Clarice was busy tinkering— she was always tinkering!—with a crystal zoometer. The vet sighed and pushed her glasses up her nose. When she noticed the girls, she instantly brightened.

"Hello, you two!"

"How's Jade doing?" asked Rosie, walking over to stroke Jade's scaly tail.

"She's on the mend," answered Doctor Clarice. "But I need your help with another problem—and urgently. There seems to be something wrong with the latest batch of mystical crystals from the Gnome Town mine."

"Mystical crysticals, you mean!" said Kat. Doctor Clarice smiled for a moment, but then she looked serious again.

"The power is draining from them too quickly. And that's a real problem, because we don't have many left. The mystical crystals usually grow as quickly as the gnomes can mine them, but recently they've stopped growing entirely."

"That's dreadful!" gasped Rosie. "Without crystals, the zoometers won't work. We won't be able to find the animals if they're sick!"

"It's even worse than that," said Doctor Clarice. "All our machines will run out of power, even our magnetoscope, which works like the x-ray machines in human hospitals. We'd never know if a hodgepodge had swallowed a spoon! And we've nearly run out of crystal fuel to power the flying carpet on rescue missions." She shook her head. "Come and see the crystal converter."

Doctor Clarice led them into the next room, where Quibble, the vet surgery's porter, was pouring crystals into the funnel of a large, clanking machine. If it had not been for Quibble's bright eyes, he could have been mistaken for a mossy tree stump, but to Kat and Rosie, he was an old friend, and they were no longer surprised by his appearance.

"Dreadful! Dreadful!" spluttered Quibble, his beard of soft green moss twitching. "The converter can only get one bucket of fuel from a whole sack of crystals. Watch!"

Kat and Rosie watched as Quibble dropped a crystal into the funnel. It whizzed and banged its way along a tube and into a wooden vat. There was a sound like someone sucking on a milkshake, then a spurt of rainbow liquid spattered out of the vat into a bucket.

"Not enough, not enough," grumbled Quibble. His bark was bristling with worry.

"It sounds like we should leave for Gnome Town right away," said Rosie. "We need to find out what's going on."

"Doctor Hart is waiting for you in the garage," nodded Doctor Clarice. "We've topped up the carpet's engine, so you should have enough fuel to get there."

Sure enough, Doctor Hart was already sitting on the carpet, which was floating just

above the ground. Rosie and Kat climbed up, and it whooshed over the treetops and away.

"Is that a lake?" asked Rosie. She was pointing at a sparkling mirror in the distance.

"It's the Frozen Lake," said Doctor Hart.

"But it looks like there are waves!"

"Of course there are! If the ice didn't move, how would the snowmaids swim through it?"

Kat glimpsed a bright fox darting between the bushes below. "Look! It's got three tails!"

"It's a kitsune," said Doctor Hart. "It's a good sign that you saw one—they're lucky."

When Kat was in Starfall Forest, she always felt lucky. But when she went home to her squabbling brothers, distracted parents, and needy baby sister ... well, that was a different story altogether.

"We aren't far now—the Rainbow River is just below us," said Doctor Hart.

"When we land," said Doctor Hart, "I will take you to meet the chief miner. She will be able to tell us about the trouble with the crystals. Once we've spoken to her, I'll see to the grufflegoat kids."

The magic carpet lowered itself on the outskirts of the town. Dozens of gnomes were bustling around, carrying bags of shopping or parcels. "This way," said Doctor Hart. She tucked the magic carpet behind a tree, and they began walking toward the middle of the town.

The gnomes seemed very friendly. "Hello, Doctor Hart!" they called. They smiled and waved as the little group walked past. Both the male and female gnomes were around the same height as Jayden and Jordan.

"Ah, here we are—this is the chief miner's office," said Doctor Hart, stopping abruptly.

She knocked on the door, which opened immediately. A female gnome came out.

"Oh my kettles and cuttlefish!" she exclaimed in surprise, her eyes widening at the human girls. "Are these Normilliams?"

"Kat, Rosie," said Doctor Hart, "this is Henrietta Halfpint. She is in charge of the crystal mines. These are my friends, Henrietta."

Henrietta vigorously shook everyone's hands. "Oh, I'm so very glad you're all here! Everything is going wrong!"

"What do you mean?" asked Doctor Hart.

"Well, first of all, the baby grufflegoats have gone missing! And secondly, the crystals at the mine have stopped growing. Even with our big new drilling machines, we can't reach enough gems!"

"I thought you used picks," said Doctor Hart, looking surprised.

"Yes, when there were more gnomes living here, we used picks and shovels. Then we started to use little drills, to speed things up. But now we're having to use bigger and bigger machines to find any crystals at all."

Doctor Hart's mouth dropped open. "Oh, my goodness! How things have changed."

"I know," said Henrietta. "And on top

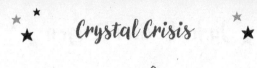

of that, we can't find the baby grufflegoats anywhere. We tucked them up in bed last night, but this morning they were nowhere to be seen!"

"Those poor things!" said Rosie.

Two gnomes hurried toward Henrietta. They had dirty smudges all over their clothes.

"Henrietta," said one, "we've investigated the deepest caves—we think there may be some bigger crystals buried deeper down—but we'll need to use the big drills."

Looking downcast, Henrietta Halfpint led the gnomes to one side. It looked as though she was telling them to use the very biggest drill. Doctor Hart had become very fidgety. "I didn't realize things were this serious."

Henrietta came back over to them. "I am going to join the search for the grufflegoats, Henrietta," said Doctor Hart.

"Thank you," said the gnome.

"Please could you take us to the mines so we can see the crystals, Miss Halfpint?" asked Kat. "Doctor Clarice says she needs some for her machines."

"I can, yes," said Henrietta. "I need to go there now anyway."

"I'll come and find you shortly,' said Doctor Hart to Kat and Rosie. Then she tottered off, looking very concerned indeed.

Henrietta handed the girls a hard hat each and led them over a footbridge that crossed the Rainbow River. A pair of small lilac songbirds swooped overhead.

"Those are chatterknitters," explained Henrietta. "We take grufflegoat wool to their nests, and they knit clothes with their beaks."

After a few minutes, they reached the dark and dusty entrance to the mine.

As soon as the girls stepped inside, they had to dodge out of the way of busy, scurrying gnomes, all in hard hats. Henrietta handed Kat a lamp, then led the girls deeper into the darkness. What struck Kat and Rosie the most was the very loud, deep rumbling sound. "That must be the drills," said Kat.

"Unfortunately, the mines aren't what they once were," said Henrietta.

Kat and Rosie exchanged a glance. They had both imagined majestic caves shining with beautiful crystals, but instead they were met with a very dingy sight. Just a handful of small crystals were dotted over the dark walls, and the air was filled with smoke and dust. The grinding of the drills was deafening.

Henrietta led them over to a pile of tiny crystals. Kat and Rosie began to search

through the heap for anything large enough to use in a zoometer. But out of the corner of her eye, Kat saw something moving in the shadows.

A dragon, around the same size as Jade, was watching them, its eyes wide.

Kat remembered that Doctor Hart had said the dragons lived in caves. But this noisy, smoky cave was a terrible place for a little dragon to live! Before Kat or Rosie could do or say anything, the dragon had scampered away down a dark tunnel.

Chapter 4
Missing Grufflegoats

*E*ager to escape the noise and smoke of the cave, Kat and Rosie filled their pockets with handfuls of the little crystals.

Henrietta Halfpint led them back to the entrance. "Don't worry, we'll find you some better crystals soon enough," she said. "We gnomes have a motto: 'Even the biggest problems have small solutions.'" And with that, she scurried back into the darkness.

Kat and Rosie sat down together on a patch of grass to wait for Doctor Hart. "I wish we could help!" said Rosie.

"Me too," said Kat. "It doesn't feel right,

having those huge machines here."

They soon saw Doctor Hart marching back across the meadow. "Nowhere to be found!" she cried. "I can't find the grufflegoats anywhere! The poor, loveable little babies!"

Kat crossed her arms tightly, feeling a sudden rush of anger. "Why does everyone think babies are cute?" she said. "They just cause trouble and make everyone run around after them."

Rosie looked surprised, but didn't say anything. Kat immediately felt embarrassed at her outburst.

"Just joking!" she said, standing up. "Can we help find the grufflegoats, Doctor Hart?"

"I haven't searched the Moonflower Meadows yet ... " the doctor replied.

Henrietta hurried over to join them. Just as she opened her mouth to speak, the noise of the drills got even louder. "Before you set off searching again," she shouted, "you really must have something to eat."

Henrietta led them to a large tree, then pulled open a door in its trunk. They all stepped into a small, cramped room. All the furniture—chairs, tables, and shelves— was curved around the inside of the tree.

"It's just like the surgery!" said Rosie.

"Well spotted, dearie," said Doctor Hart. "They look similar because the surgery was built by gnomes."

Henrietta disappeared up a twisting staircase, just as a male gnome emerged from another door. He was wearing a sweater and overalls. "Hello, I'm Henrietta's brother, Rufus! Please sit down!" he squeaked.

He set down some very small cups, then poured some bright green juice out of a teapot. He offered them a plate of sandwiches.

Henrietta reappeared, wearing a pretty dress and with moonflowers in her hair.

Doctor Hart, Kat, and Rosie were hungry and tired, so they ate and drank gratefully. The green juice tasted of strawberries. "Your house is wonderful!" said Rosie, loudly.

"You are too kind!" shouted Rufus. At this, his sweater changed from light orange to blush pink.

"Your sweater!" exclaimed Kat excitedly.

"Yes!" said Rufus. "It is made from grufflegoat wool. You cannot find a warmer material anywhere. And it magically changes to show your mood! Just now it's pink, because I feel proud."

"That's amazing!" replied Kat, taking another sip of the juice. The noise of the drills stopped at last.

Rufus looked down at his sweater, which had changed again. "And now it's

yellow, because I'm happy that the noise has stopped!"

The girls laughed at that. They were relieved, too. What a din the drills made!

"The sweaters help the gnomes to look after each other," said Doctor Hart, "because they can tell how everyone is feeling. Red means angry, orange means curious, blue means scared ... you'll learn soon enough!"

"Would you girls like to try one on?" asked Rufus, holding up a sweater.

"Oh yes!" said Rosie at once.

Kat wasn't so sure. Her emotions had been unpredictable recently, and she didn't know if she wanted to share them with everyone.

Rosie put on the sweater first. The wool was very soft and thick. After a few seconds it turned a mellow yellow, like sunflower petals.

"You must feel quite happy, then, Rosie," said Rufus.

"I guess I am!" said Rosie cheerfully, looking down at her arm. "This must be what people mean when they talk about wearing your heart on your sleeve."

"Your turn, Kat," said Rufus.

Rosie took off the sweater and passed it over. Kat reluctantly pulled it on. Almost at once, the material flushed red.

"A little … frustration, I suppose?" said Henrietta, kindly.

"Maybe a bit," said Kat. She gulped. "I'm a bit annoyed with my family," she managed.

Henrietta looked concerned, but she nodded. "That's very normal, it's something lots of us go through as we grow up."

"Yesterday was our special movie night," said Kat, "but Dad forgot about it completely. No one has any time for me any more."

Now the sweater had turned violet.

"Let me guess—violet for embarrassment, right?" said Kat. She could feel tears starting to prick her eyes. "Would it be okay if I went out for some fresh air?"

"Yes, my dear," said Doctor Hart, knowing that Kat needed a few moments to herself. "We'll be out in a few minutes. Don't go far."

Kat stepped outside, closing the door in

the tree trunk behind her. She drifted into the meadow, where the noise of the drills was fainter.

She saw a little well with flowers growing around it. "A wishing well," she murmured. She walked down a pebbled path toward it. "I could wish for everything to go back to the way it was before."

The moment she had said it out loud, Kat looked around in shock, as if someone else had spoken. Was that really how she felt?

She perched on the edge of the well, thinking about how her father used to take her to the park, and how her mother used to braid her hair.

A hot feeling bubbled in her chest. She looked at her reflection in the well. Her face was scowling, and her sweater was so red it was almost glowing.

Kat reached into her pocket and found a coin. It was the only one she had left—she had given the rest to the hodgepodge.

"Maybe I *do* wish for the baby to disappear, and for everything to return to how it was before … " Kat said.

She felt like she wanted this, but it also made her feel uneasy—as though it wasn't what she really needed at all. It was very confusing. Really, she wanted her parents back, and to not feel so mad all the time. She held the coin out over the water and thought about dropping it—but as she looked down at the water her reflection changed.

For a split second she saw herself holding Brianna. The baby was laughing happily—and so was Kat. The rest of her family looked on, smiling. Kat gasped and jumped back. "What am I thinking!"

she cried. She swung around and hurried back toward Rufus, Henrietta, and Rosie. But after a few quick steps, she stumbled. "What was that?" asked Kat—she had tripped over something. Then, to her amazement two small eyes blinked at her.

"Woah!" she cried, about to dash away, when she noticed that the eyes belonged to the outline of animal shaped like ...

"A grufflegoat!" Kat shouted. As she looked closer, she could see that it had green legs and a sandy-yellow body and face—it was perfectly camouflaged against the path and the grass in the meadow!

Kat knelt down near the grufflegoat and reached out a hand. It made a little bleating sound and trotted toward her. "Okay, I'll admit it," said Kat. "You are pretty adorable. Have you been hiding out here?"

The drills had briefly fallen quiet, but now they started up with a roar, and the baby grufflegoat leaped onto Kat's lap, quivering.

Its coat changed to a worried light blue. "You poor little thing. Where are the other baby grufflegoats?" Kat asked.

At this, the goat bounded across the field. Kat watched as it came to a stop by the well. Then she saw dozens more eyes blinking at her.

Kat raced to Henrietta's house and knocked on the door. "They're here!" she shouted. "The grufflegoats are hiding by the wishing well! I think they ran away from the noisy drills."

Doctor Hart, Henrietta, Rufus, and Rosie rushed outside—and when they saw that Kat had found the goats, they were overjoyed.

"Thank you, thank you!" said Rufus and Henrietta as they cuddled the grufflegoats.

Henrietta gave Kat a handful of rainbow-striped berries to feed to the goats, and the babies gobbled them up happily.

Henrietta's dress and Rufus' sweater were glowing the brightest yellow. Looking down, Kat saw that her own top had also taken on a golden hue.

She shrugged the sweater off, all the same. She didn't need people to know what she was feeling *all* the time.

While Rosie and Henrietta were talking, Rufus moved a bit closer to Kat.

"You found the well, didn't you?" he said quietly. "Most people don't even notice it. But if you were drawn to it, something must have been troubling you a great deal."

"I, I was thinking ... that life would be easier without my baby sister ... " she said. "But then the well showed me a happy picture of us all together. What does it mean? Is it a wishing well?"

"It's actually a well-wishing well. Rather

than granting wishes, it helps you turn your thoughts around, so that you don't have to make the wish in the first place."

This gave Kat lots to think about. A grufflegoat baby bounded onto her lap and nuzzled into her neck affectionately. She stroked its wool, which gave off a sunny, golden glow.

Chapter 5
Into the Lair

A few days later, Kat stifled an enormous yawn as she knocked on the door to Willow Cottage. Brianna had cried all night, and everyone had been grumpy at breakfast. Her father had snapped at Jordan and Jayden for climbing on the bookcases, and then her mother had got mad at him, too.

She tried to remember the happy picture that the well-wishing well had shown her, but it was so difficult.

Rosie's mother answered. "Hello, Kat. Rosie's just finishing her piano lesson. Would you like a juice?"

"Oh, yes please," said Kat.

They sat down in the kitchen. "How are things at home?" asked Rosie's mother kindly.

Kat was about to say everything was fine, but then she remembered the bright red sweater. Maybe it was better to talk about feelings, rather than just bottling them up.

"It's tough," managed Kat. "Brianna makes everyone so bad-tempered."

"Oh, sweetheart," said Rosie's mother, "I remember when my sister Marie was born, I wished she would just disappear!" She chuckled. "I promise it will get better."

Kat felt a lot better for talking. So much so that by the time Rosie came out of her piano lesson, all she could think about was getting into the forest and finding out how Jade was doing.

"We're off to see the dragon!" sang Rosie, as they skipped into the garden.

"Sure you are. Tell it I said hello!" her mother replied with a laugh.

Kat and Rosie giggled as they raced into the trees—until they stumbled across a creature rustling about in the bushes. "Stop!" said Kat. "Look! It's a boombadger."

A large green creature was shaking the branches. They could just make out the square patchwork pattern on its back between the leaves. Rosie tiptoed over to get a better look, but as she drew closer, the creature tumbled out of its bush. It looked up at her.

"Quick! Run!" called Kat, laughing as the boombadger's fur stood on end. A great cloud of stinking green smoke exploded from the creature.

"Yuck!" laughed Rosie, holding her nose. "Rotten eggs!" They ran as fast as they could.

"They'd make great pets," laughed Rosie, "if it weren't for one small thing!"

When the girls reached the surgery, they headed straight to see Jade. They found Doctor Clarice polishing her scales. Half were a dull, muddy green, while the rest were shining brilliantly like emeralds. "Hello, girls," said Clarice, looking up. "Lovely to see you. Our friend here is doing much better."

"Oh wow," said Kat, as she neared the dragon. "That green is beautiful."

"Yes," said Doctor Clarice. "She's not been

cleaning herself properly, which is a sign of unhappiness. We've been taking good care of her and she's slowly perking up. This little collywobble has been keeping her company."

Kat knew this was a perfect job for a collywobble, as they liked nothing more than cuddles. The furry little creature was stroking Jade with his long, feathered tail.

The dragon opened her eyes and looked lovingly at Doctor Clarice, who petted her chin. "I've been feeding her berries—she loves them."

Doctor Morel bustled through the door. "Hello, girls! Thank you for finding our lost grufflegoats last week!"

"You are very welcome," said Kat.

"Doctor Clarice," said the gnome, "we have a few topplebottom birds with headaches— could you take a look at them?"

"Those silly birds," smiled Doctor Clarice. "Why do they insist on building their nests upside down?"

"We could polish the dragon's scales while you're gone," said Rosie, shyly.

"That would be fantastic!" said Doctor Clarice. "I won't be long. Here, take these grufflegoat-wool cloths and wipe her scales nice and gently."

Rosie picked up a cloth and moved closer to the dragon. She gave the collywobble a gentle stroke as she sat down. Its fur was beautifully soft.

Together, Kat and Rosie worked away, polishing Jade's scales until they all shone brightly. "She loves it!" laughed Rosie, as the dragon made more and more happy sounds.

Kat noticed that some of the little crystals they had collected from the gnomes' mine were on a table nearby. As Jade purred, the crystals seemed to glow.

Kat went over to take a closer look. The crystals were quivering and making a faint hum. "Look Rosie!" said Kat, "the crystals are vibrating. And … I … think they may have grown a bit too!"

"That's amazing!" said Rosie.

When Doctor Clarice returned, Jade the dragon stood up and stretched.

"Oh, she is feeling better!" smiled Clarice. "Thank you, girls."

"Doctor Clarice ... " said Kat, "I noticed that as we were polishing Jade's scales, and she was beginning to feel better, the crystals began glowing and humming. They even grew a tiny bit bigger!"

"Really?" said Doctor Clarice, surprised. "Now that *is* interesting."

"Can we do anything else?" asked Rosie.

"Well, Doctor Hart is going to take Jade home now. She is well enough, and it's time she rejoined her family in the caves at Cottontop Mountains. Would you like to go with her?"

"Yes of course!" they said in unison.

"Here, Kat, take a crystal with you," said Doctor Clarice. "See if you notice anything else strange."

The collywobble snuffled anxiously at Jade the dragon's tail.

"Aaah, when a collywobble makes a friend, they find it hard to say goodbye," said Doctor Clarice. "Don't worry, little collywobble. We'll take you to visit your dragon friend soon."

Within a few moments, Kat, Rosie, Jade, and Doctor Hart were all on board the magic carpet. Jade looked around at the passing clouds and trees, watching with interest. They flew over the Mazewood in the direction of Gnome Town, but when they reached the Rainbow River, the magic carpet swerved sharply and changed direction.

"What's happening?" said Rosie. She could see the rooftops of Gnome Town moving

farther away—they were now flying over Moonflower Meadow toward the Crystal Caves.

Doctor Hart looked at the dragon. She could feel magic in the air. "I think Jade has decided to drive us home herself!"

They passed the gnomes' mine, a cloud of smoke marking the spot, and flew higher, getting closer to the peaks of the snow-capped mountains. "It's getting chilly!" said Kat.

At those words, the carpet began to slow down. It swooped toward an opening in the hill, on the other side of the mountain from the mine. They all expected the carpet to land—but no—Jade kept it moving and they flew straight into a cave.

As soon as their eyes adjusted to the darkness, they all gasped. They had entered a beautiful cave lined with dazzling crystals.

"Just look at these gems!" laughed Kat. "They're what I'd call *real* mystical crysticals!"

"Wonderful!" said Doctor Hart. "This gives me hope!"

"Wait—" shouted Rosie. "What are those shapes ... are they ... dragons?"

In the dim light, they could make out a number of dragon-shaped shadows. With a determined expression on her face, Jade lowered the carpet gently to the ground. Doctor Hart and the girls got off and moved cautiously closer to the creatures— they had found a group of very sick dragons.

"I'm sorry to say that they all have dragon flu," said Doctor Hart, after she had quickly examined the creatures. "We can't take them all back to the surgery—we're going to have to get Doctor Clarice and set up a field hospital right here."

As Doctor Hart spoke, they heard the buzz of the gnomes' drills through the rock of the mountain, and caught a whiff of smoke.

Jade had been standing to the side, watching. Now, she dashed around the other dragons, and then back to the humans.

"I think I understand," said Doctor Hart. "Yes, of course we'll help your family."

Chapter 6
Crystal Chaos

$\mathcal{T}$ he next morning, as her brothers raced their toy cars over the kitchen counter, Kat got out her notebook to jot down her thoughts about the dragons, crystals, and drills. She felt like she was close to a discovery. Kat saw Brianna looking at her, so she showed the baby some drawings of dragons. Brianna looked delighted, and Kat's heart swelled.

Jayden drove his car up Mama's arm and over baby Brianna's face. Brianna started wailing. "Jayden, please stop!" said Mama tiredly, rocking the red-faced baby in her arms. Brianna's wailing grew louder.

Now Kat couldn't think at all. "So much noise!" she wrote. How could she make a plan when she couldn't think straight?

Then she stared at the words in her notebook. "Feelings ... dragons ... crystals ... noise ... oh!" Suddenly, she gasped.

"I'm off to Rosie's house, Mama!" she called over her shoulder, as she rushed out of the door. She couldn't wait to share her breakthrough with her best friend.

Kat explained her idea to Rosie, and the girls set off excitedly for the vets' surgery. But when they got there, Doctor Hart was very busy, getting the magic carpet ready to leave.

"Are we going to check on the dragons?" asked Rosie, as she and Kat climbed aboard.

"Not just now, dearies," answered Doctor Hart. "Since those sick dragons need care around the clock, I've called in help from the vets at Crinklecrag Woods and Fairydust Forest. But we must hurry to Gnome Town. It's more important than ever that we find more crystals for our machines."

When the carpet landed at the gnomes' mine, they saw a great commotion. Henrietta and Rufus were standing among a crowd of angry gnomes. "There are no crystals left!" they yelled, "What are we going to do?"

"Everyone stay calm!" shouted Henrietta.

"Panicking won't help anyone. We'll just have to start drilling through the night, too. We'll find more crystals eventually."

Now the girls noticed an enormous new drilling machine. "That looks like the drills I saw on construction sites back when I lived in Opal City," said Rosie. "They're so loud!"

A gnome revved the engine to show everyone how powerful it was. The noise made the ground shake.

"This is terrible! I must speak to Henrietta at once," cried Doctor Hart.

Rosie clutched her pounding head. "Let's get away from the noise," she said to Kat.

They strode away from the crowd and into the meadow. "That's better," said Rosie as they heard the drill stop.

Kat felt something moving in her pocket. She pulled out the crystal Doctor Clarice had given her the day before. It was glowing.

"This means I was right!" she said, excitedly. They raced back to the mine. "Doctor Hart, Henrietta, Rufus—we've made a discovery."

The adults had been arguing, but now they turned to face her. "Yes, my dear—what is it?" said Doctor Hart.

"Well," said Kat, holding out the crystal in the palm of her hand. "When we were looking after Jade, we noticed the crystals glittering and growing, but it only happened when she was happy."

Henrietta's eyes grew wide. "Go on."

"The same thing happened here when the drilling stopped," said Kat. "We think the cystals are just like the grufflegoats' wool—they respond to feelings."

"Feelings? Whose feelings?" said Henrietta.

"The dragons'!" said Kat, "You need to stop drilling, because it's making them sad."

"You may well be right," said Rufus, "but we can't just go back to using picks and shovels. We have to live in the real world."

"There must be something we can do,"
whispered Kat to Rosie, who nodded back.

Later, when they had returned to the
vets' surgery, Kat explained her theory to
Doctor Clarice.

"I think you're absolutely right," said
Doctor Clarice. "It's going to be very difficult
to get the gnomes to stop drilling, though.
They rely on the crystals for their livelihood."

Kat looked serious. "If we can't get them to stop making all that noise, then maybe we can protect the dragons somehow." She had images in her head of dragons wearing fluffy earmuffs.

"Hmmm," said Doctor Clarice. She was thinking so hard, she'd actually stopped tinkering with her gadgets. "Well, it's nearly egg-laying season, so we'll have to make sure the dragons get better very soon."

Kat and Rosie both cried, "We can help!"

"Thank you, sweethearts," said Doctor Clarice. "The kind vets from Crinklecrag are with the dragons right now. But tomorrow morning it's our turn to care for them. If you get here nice and early tomorrow, we can take the flying carpet straight to the dragon lair to care for them."

"We will! We promise!" chorused the girls.

After saying their goodbyes, Kat and Rosie headed for Willow Cottage, where they found Rosie's parents gardening. "Another good afternoon playing, girls?" asked Rosie's dad.

"Yes, thanks!" said Kat.

"Would you like to stay for dinner, Kat?" he asked.

"Yes, please," said Kat. "But may I call home to check that it's okay?"

"Go ahead."

Kat found the phone in the hallway. It rang for a long time before she heard her mother's voice answer, "Hello?"

"Hi. Please can I have dinner at Rosie's?"

"Yes, Kat—that sounds perfect, actually. I haven't managed to get to the supermarket to buy anything for dinner."

Although Kat was glad she was allowed to stay, she couldn't help feeling a little hurt

that her mother was so pleased that she wouldn't be coming home for dinner.

During the meal, Kat and Rosie explained the problem with the dragons and the drills. Rosie's parents thought they had amazing imaginations!

"Why don't you let the gnomes meet Jade?" said Rosie's mother, with a big smile. "It's not so easy to forget the effect our actions have on others once we get to know them."

Chapter 7
Baby Dragons

*W*hen the girls arrived at the surgery early the next morning, they found Doctor Clarice doing her rounds.

The vet was tending to a kitsune that had bruised one of its tails. Doctor Clarice was whispering soothingly to the little fox while rubbing in an ointment that smelled strongly of apple pie.

The girls explained Rosie's mother's suggestion.

Doctor Clarice nodded. "Your mother is smart, Rosie. It *is* easier to ignore people's feelings until we see them for ourselves.

If we can encourage the gnomes to love and care for the dragons ... it just might work. I've finished my duties here, so let's head for the dragons' lair right now."

They made their way to the magic carpet. A cluster of flutterpuffs jumped onboard just as it was taking off. "I guess you are coming too," giggled Rosie, as she picked one up and stroked it.

"The thing is, dragons can be very shy," said Doctor Clarice, as they flew over the Rainbow River. "It might take some coaxing to get Jade to go to Gnome Town. And ... the gnomes might be afraid of her."

The dragons' lair looked quite different from their last visit. The crystals were glowing less brightly, and by each sick

dragon there was a small, smoky fire. Kat and Rosie spotted Jade immediately—she was the only dragon standing up and moving around. Her scales weren't gleaming quite as brightly as before, though.

Jade looked very pleased to see them all. She trotted over to a corner of the cave, then waited for them to follow. When they drew closer, they saw a mother dragon cradling two tiny, wriggling creatures with her tail.

"Baby dragons!" cried Rosie.

The young dragons looked just like their mother but much tinier. They were so young, they were still resting in their shells.

"Luckily," said Doctor Clarice, stroking the mother's forehead, "this dragon isn't as sick as some of the others. And her two babies are perfectly healthy."

Kat felt Jade's warm breath on her neck. She tickled the dragon under her chin. "Jade, will you come to Gnome Town with us?" she asked. "If the gnomes see that the drilling makes you unhappy, and understand that it makes you and your friends sick—we might be able to get them to stop."

The dragon yawned loudly and lay down on the ground as if to say, "It's no use."

Then, all of a sudden there was a loud, low rumble. The gnomes must have started up the big drills, because the whole mountain was shaking! A few of the dragons made high-pitched noises. Jade stood up and shook her head angrily. Puffs of smoke billowed from her nostrils. Then, as the baby dragons started to wail, Jade launched herself into the air, soaring toward the exit on her shining wings. She looked over her shoulder to check her

human friends were following.

Kat, Rosie, and Doctor Clarice jumped on to the magic carpet, which sped off after Jade. "Wooooah!" cried Rosie, as the carpet swerved around the mountain.

There was a crowd of gnomes gathered just inside the mine. As the carpet thumped onto the ground, Henrietta, Rufus, and the others jumped back in surprise. Jade climbed atop a boulder and opened her wings fiercely. She blew a puff of angry smoke.

The new drill was boring into the mountainside. Kat and Rosie clapped their hands over their ears to keep out the terrible noise. The ground was shaking and dust was rising into the sky.

Poor Jade was becoming more and more desperate. Her scales were darkening and her wings were trembling. Then, she gave a tremendous sneeze. The spurt of flame just missed Rufus' beard.

"What on Earth is happening?" Henrietta called to Doctor Clarice. They could only just hear her over the noise of the drill.

Jade was flapping her wings and stamping her feet.

"Oh, the poor thing!" gasped Rosie.

"Stop!" yelled Kat. "Stop the drill—can't you see? The noise is hurting her!"

Then Jade made a leap for the drill itself,

flying through the air on her green wings. She climbed into the drill's cabin and jabbed with her nose at the controls. Finally, she took a lever in her mouth and tried to pull it.

Henrietta look horrified—she strode over to the drill, climbed into the cabin beside Jade, and pulled the lever for the little dragon. The machine turned off.

Jade lay down on the ground, exhausted by her effort.

Kat, Rosie, and Doctor Clarice dashed to Jade to comfort her. Henrietta and Rufus gazed down at the unhappy dragon.

Kat took Doctor Clarice's crystal from her pocket and laid it in front of the dragon on a rock. "Please watch this," she said to the confused gnomes.

"What exactly are we looking at?" asked Henrietta. A number of the other gnomes

were crowding around inquisitively.

"The crystal," said Kat. "Watch—as Jade gets happier, the crystal will grow."

Kat and Rosie stroked Jade's scales and smoothed her wings. Jade rolled over onto her back, enjoying the attention from her two friends. As the dragon gave a purr, the crystal began to vibrate and hum.

More gnomes were gathering to watch now. They whispered to each other and pointed at the crystal. Doctor Clarice began to tickle Jade's feet. At this, the humming crystal became noticeably bigger.

"But what does this mean?" called one of the miners. "Does this mean we should bring the dragons here?"

"We will need to hold a meeting," said Henrietta, holding her arms out wide, "and discuss all our options."

"Well," said an angry-looking gnome at the front of the crowd, "I need to get back to work. I have a family to feed!" And with that, he marched back over to the new drill, climbed aboard, and turned it on.

Everyone covered their ears at once. Before anyone had even had a chance to move, the drill made an ear-piercing screech. "I've lost control!" cried the gnome driving it. "Help!"

"Quick, girls, get Jade out of the way," shouted Doctor Clarice. But the ground—and the mountain itself—was shaking violently.

"Oh no!" called Henrietta. She was pointing at the rocks above the mine entrance. The mountainside was crumbling!

Everyone ran into the mine entrance for shelter, Jade scrambling alongside them. They were not a moment too soon.

With a terrible roar, rock after rock crashed to the ground just outside. The entrance was blocked!

"We're stuck!" called a gnome.

Henrietta ordered that the other entrances to the mine be checked immediately.

Kat and Rosie held each other tightly. In all their adventures in the forest they had never felt truly scared. But now they were stuck, with no way of getting home!

"What will my family think if I don't come home tonight?" thought Kat. She thought of her parents looking at the clock as they fed her little brothers. She thought about the baby crying while her mother called Rosie's parents to see where she was, only to be told that they didn't know either. Kat squeezed Rosie's hand. Rosie squeezed back, but she looked worried.

The gnomes returned from checking the other entrances, but they had very bad news.

"Everything is blocked!" the gnomes cried.

The gnomes began rushing around, shouting in panicked voices, until Jade let out a loud squawk. The noise echoed around the cave, which made everyone stop and look at her. Jade began pacing up and down. She was looking at the roof of the mine.

"Has she seen something?" asked Rosie.

"I'm not sure," said Kat. "Wait—yes she has!" Jade was motioning to her and Rosie to climb onto her back.

"Should we?" said Rosie nervously, but Kat ran over and pulled herself up. "Come on!" she shouted. "She wants to take us somewhere!"

Once Rosie was settled on Jade's back with her arms around Kat's waist, Jade took off.

"Maybe she knows a way out!" said Kat.

"Be careful!" called Doctor Clarice.

Kat gripped Jade's scales tightly and both girls leaned in close to the dragon's body. Together they flew up, until they were very close to the roof of the cave. The gnomes and Doctor Clarice were watching nervously from below.

"Look," said Rosie. "She's taking us to that ledge."

Jade flew swiftly to the wall of the cave and settled on a small, overhanging slab of rock. Behind it was an opening. "I think it's a passageway," said Kat, as she carefully climbed off Jade's back to have a look.

"Be careful!" called Rosie, as Kat took a few steps inside.

"I can hear birds!" she called. "This must be a way out."

"Thank you, Jade," said Rosie, wrapping

her arms around the dragon's neck. "Thank you! Thank you!"

Kat called down to Doctor Clarice and Henrietta: "There's a way out up here!"

Cheers broke out below.

"The dragon has saved us!" a gnome cried.

"We have to take care of the dragons!" cried another.

Kat and Rosie smiled.

Chapter 8
The Great Escape

Jade flew down and picked up Doctor Clarice before quickly returning to the ledge. Together, Kat, Rosie, and Clarice began feeling their way along the passage to find their way out, with Jade leading the way. Behind them, the gnomes began climbing on each other's shoulders, making a kind of gnome-ladder to reach the ledge. There was a lot of huffing and puffing.

"They'll pull each other up," Doctor Clarice explained.

The passageway was very dark, but Kat had been right—they could hear noises

from outside the mine. There was birdsong, as well as the tinkling of running water.

"I'm not certain," said Doctor Clarice, "but I think that this passageway is going to bring us out by the Crystal Falls."

She was right. Quite soon, the path began sloping upward and the ground became wet. The passageway slowly grew brighter, until they stepped out into daylight. They were standing on a rock platform behind a beautiful waterfall.

"Look!" said Kat. She was pointing along the cliff at a narrow ledge that ran behind the waterfall. "There's a way out!"

"Oh that looks dangerous!" said Rosie.

But Kat, Rosie and Doctor Clarice carefully edged their way along, while Jade flew through the waterfall. She looked like she was having a lot of fun as she splashed and rolled in the water.

It was a short but steep walk back to the mine entrance. When they arrived, they found a crowd of worried-looking gnomes trying to dig their way through the rubble. Doctor Morel was there helping to clear the rocks onto a cart pulled by some grown-up grufflegoats.

"Cats and cabbages, am I ever glad to see you safe!" he exclaimed on seeing the girls.

Doctor Clarice explained what had

happened, and when she told them that Jade had shown them a way out, a dozen gnomes came up to the dragon and hugged her tightly. Jade purred with pleasure.

Then, to everyone's surprise, some little pink crystals popped up among the broken rocks. They were sparkling.

"Oh wow," said Kat and Rosie.

"When the dragons feel loved ... the crystals grow," said Doctor Clarice under her breath.

Eventually, all the gnomes that had been trapped inside made it through the passageway and back to their friends. Henrietta apologized, over and over again, to Doctor Clarice, Kat, and Rosie.

Jade had started to look restless. Finally, she took to the air and flew in the direction of the dragons' lair. As usual, she kept looking over her shoulder to check that her friends were following her. Doctor Clarice, Kat, and Rosie climbed onto the magic carpet and sped off behind the dragon.

At the dragons' lair, everything was peaceful. The drills were silent. All the dragons looked like they had recovered from their flu. Their scales were shining and no sneezing could be heard.

The girls soon noticed that four or five more eggs had hatched while they had been gone. Jade padded over to greet the new arrivals. As she sniffed the babies' shining scales, the crystals all around began to hum and glow with a rainbow of sparkling light. As the babies played and tumbled together, shining crystals popped up all around the mother dragons.

"Come, girls," murmured Doctor Clarice, not wanting to disturb the babies. "If I keep you any later, your parents will be worried."

For the first time in weeks, Kat realized she wanted to go home. All the way back on the flying carpet and through the woods, she could not wait to see her family—even baby Brianna. When they were stuck in the cave, all she had thought about was Mama, Dad, the twins, and Brianna.

"Hello!" she called as she opened the front door to her house.

She heard Brianna's crying coming from the family room. She rushed in, finding Mama jiggling the baby on her hip and the twins climbing over the sofa. Her mother smiled warmly on seeing her.

Kat gave her mother a big hug. "Can I hold Brianna, Mama?" she asked.

"Yes, thank you," said her mother, surprised. "My arms could do with a rest."

Jade took baby Brianna. She felt warm and soft, and surprisingly heavy. Kat jigged  gently from foot to foot, like she had seen her parents do. After a few moments, Brianna stopped crying and gurgled. It was working!

"Mama, she's stopped crying!" Kat whispered. But her mother was already fast asleep on the sofa. Kat and Brianna smiled at each other. Kat knew she would never ever want Brianna to disappear again.

Chapter 9
A Chocolate Cake

The next afternoon, Kat and Rosie were enjoying the best chocolate cake they had ever tasted. Henrietta and Rufus had invited the girls and Doctor Clarice to their tree house for a snack. They wanted to say thank you for the girls' discovery about the drills.

Rufus told them the secret chocolate cake recipe was passed down from gnome father to gnome son. Kat noticed that when the cake first melted on her tongue, she tasted rich, sticky chocolate. Then there was a fizz of raspberry, followed by a twist of apricot. She had never tasted anything so delicious.

"On behalf of all the gnomes," said Henrietta, "I cannot thank you girls enough."

"You're very welcome," said Rosie happily, taking another bite of cake.

"Once we are back in the mine and it's safe, we will look at other ways of mining," continued Henrietta. "The biggest drill isn't safe to use at all. And now I understand that the dragons make the crystals, we'll find a way to care for the dragons too."

"Yes," agreed Rufus, "the poor dragons."

"However, in the meantime, we will go back to using the smaller drills for a few hours each day," said Henrietta.

Kat and Rosie leaped up in surprise. How could Henrietta say that, after everything that had happened?

"I thought you understood!" exclaimed Kat. "The dragons need ... "

"That's just it," said Henrietta, firmly. "The dragons need it to be peaceful, but the gnomes need to be able to feed their families. Until we have a new way of getting to the crystals, we have to keep drilling."

"Wait—" said Kat. "There must be some other way." She had to speak quite loudly as the gnomes had started up a few machines to clear the rubble from the mine entrance.

"Well," said Henrietta, "we used to dig with picks, but it took a lot of gnomes and a very long time. Sometimes we would dig for days without finding any mystical crystals at all. The drills are twenty times faster. We just drill away chunks of rock, then carry it outside to smash with hammers."

"But—" began Kat.

"Girls," said Doctor Clarice. She shook her head at Kat. "It's time we headed back to the surgery to check on our injured kitsune."

Kat nodded.

As the magic carpet swept over the treetops, Kat thought about the gnomes. If they couldn't find more crystals quickly, they would soon go back to using bigger drills. "If only gnomes could find magical things as quickly as hodgepodges," she thought to herself. "Wait—that's it!"

"What's it?" asked Rosie, startled.

"Hodgepodges!" answered Kat. "They could help the gnomes find crystals. And they love to dig and burrow!"

"They do," said Doctor Clarice. "But hodgepodges don't like to give up their magical treasure, so they would hide the crystals in their nests."

"But I know what they love even more than treasure," said Kat, smiling. Rufus had given Kat another slice of cake to take home, and she waved it in the air triumphantly.

"Chocolate!" shouted Rosie.

As the carpet touched down, Kat and Rosie ran out into the forest with their cake. When they found the beech tree where the hodgepodge nests had been, it was empty.

Kat knelt down and unwrapped her cake. "I've got chocolate!" she called sweetly.

First one, then two, then four furry hodgepodges scampered out of a hole between the roots of a nearby tree.

"Would you like some?" asked Kat, offering each hodgepodge a chunk of cake. They gobbled up the snack, licked their lips, and opened their mouths for more.

"I know some gnomes who will make you chocolate cake every day, if you just help them find some sparkly, magical crystals. Would you like that?" said Kat.

The hodgepodges chattered excitedly, clapping their paws together.

"Look who's here," said Rosie happily.

Jade was trotting through the trees toward them, her green scales shining.

"Jade, the hodgepodges want to help us. Will you give us all a lift back to the mine?" asked Rosie.

Jade purred happily, showering little pink crystals over the grass. She knelt down to let everyone climb onto her back.

As soon as Jade landed at the mine, the hodgepodges set to work. Each dug a tunnel with its tough little feet, sending up puffs of dust and pebbles behind them.

Within moments, the muddy hodgepodges returned. Each one was proudly carrying a beautiful shining crystal.

Rosie rewarded every hodgepodge with a bite of her cake.

The gnomes gathered around, calling to each other and clapping their hands with joy. Henrietta and Rufus soon joined them.

"Oh my!" gasped Henrietta. "We will never need drills again. You've saved us all! The gnomes, the dragons—all the magical creatures!"

"I'd better start baking another chocolate cake!" laughed Rufus.

Kat and Rosie giggled.

"Aha!" said Henrietta. "The chatterknitters have a gift for you." She pointed to the sky.

A flock of lilac birds was fluttering toward them, holding two grufflegoat sweaters in their beaks. Every so often, one of the birds lost its hold as it opened its mouth to chatter.

The birds placed the sweaters over Kat and Rosie's heads. The girls couldn't help laughing. The wool turned a deep pink.

"Look!" called Henrietta. There, flying among the clouds, circling and swooping, was Jade and one of her dragon friends, each wearing a sweater. "They're all better!"

Kat and Rosie's sweaters both turned a joyful yellow. Far above them, Jade the Gem Dragon's sweater turned yellow to match.

Starfall Forest Map